The Painting Day

Written by Fay Johnston
Illustrated by Heather Macallan

There was once a little girl who needed something new to do.

"I think," said her mother, "that you might like to paint."

"Ooh, yes!" said the little girl.

2

Her mother opened a cupboard
and took out a big orange can
and an old blue beach bucket.

3

She put a spoon into the can
and scooped lots of dusty orange powder
into the bucket.

She put in some water
and stirred it with a big, fat paintbrush.

She found a very big piece of paper
and pinned it to the easel.

She took the little girl outside
and handed her the brush.

She stood the easel up
and put the bucket of bright orange paint
on the ground next to it.

"What shall I paint?" asked the little girl.

"Oh," said her mother,
"you could paint some flowers, or a tree,
or a cat, or a dog.
You could even paint yourself."
Then she went inside.

The little girl looked around.

There were some yellow flowers
growing out of a crack in the sidewalk.
She painted them.
It didn't take long, and she was very proud.

There was a new little tree
that had been planted in the lawn.
It had long, curling leaves.
The little girl couldn't paint all of it,
so she just did some of the leaves.

She started to paint the house,
but it really was too big.

She started to paint the cat,
but he ran away and sat on the roof
of the big shed.

The neighbor's dog came to visit.
He was nice.
He sat very still while the little girl
painted his soft floppy ears.

Then she painted a beautiful orange stripe
down his back,
and some big dots on his tail.

Before the little girl had time
to start painting herself,
her mother came out with an apple for her.

Her mother looked at the big sheet of white paper.

"Oh, what a shame!" she said.
"You haven't painted anything!"